THE EYE OF THE C⊙RE

A Chronicle of the Cloudarians

THE EYE OF THE CORE

A Chronicle of the Cloudarians

BY NATASHA BEDDINGFIELD

LOWBAR
PUBLISHING COMPANY

905 South Douglas Avenue • Nashville, Tennessee 37204
Phone: 615-972-2842 • Web site: www.Lowbarbookstore.com
E-mail: Lowbarpublishingcompany@gmail.com

Lowbar Publishing Company
905 S. Douglas Ave.
Nashville, Tennessee 37204
615-972-2842
Lowbarpublishingcompany@gmail.com
www.Lowbarbookstore.com

Author: Natasha Beddingfield
Editor: Michelle Ben
Writer: Calvin C. Barlow, Jr.
Format Artist: Norah S. Branch
Graphic and Cover Design Artist: Norah S. Branch

Printed in the United States of America
ISBN: 978-1-7329202-4-8

For additional information or to contact the author for workshops or seminars, please email the author at nash2tag@gmail.com or Lowbar Publishing Company

Table of Contents

CHAPTERS

1 The Burden of Being Privileged 1

2 The Night That Changed My Life 10

3 My First Experience of Adulthood 16

4 A Taste of Love..25

5 A Ceremony of Life's Assignment 31

6 Crunch Time 36

7 Love and Illness 41

8 The Ecstasies of Earth 50

9   The Unexpected Invasion 86

10   A Journey to the Core 95

11   Truth and Its Consequences 116

12   The Sacrifice of Being Privileged.................119

The Main Characters

Princess Airea Dorm

Marenea

Themar Lounce

Bilow

Prince Latherius

King Con

Daisy

Hunter

Prima

Harie Pouple

Doctor Taron

Whiley

Turin

Youf

Vos

Midgle

Hundu

Tori

The Burden of Being Privileged

---

*I*t felt like yesterday! My mother was telling me bedtime stories about the origin of the Cloudarians. Marenea, my nanny, would attempt to emulate my mom's expressions, but no one could match her animation and uncanny ability to excite people with words. She began by telling me that The Core created the Cloudarians. We were hidden from humans to maintain a balance within the earth's atmosphere. When God created the earth, He left a mystical power behind, called "The Core". The Cloudarians lived in a sphere within the earth's life cycle. She would get excited when she would describe the purpose of our people's appointment by The Core.

It was hard to believe I'd grown from a little princess to turning eighteen in two days! As I contemplated the possibilities of my life, I heard a chime on my aerial. Before I got the chance to answer, Themar burst into my room with a wild smile on her face. I knew my best friend. She was probably more excited about my maturity date than I was. Since she turned eighteen years of age, her maturity day had been a frequent conversation. She had been planning, over a year, a list of things we could do together once I became eighteen. However, I did not know, but I had a weary feeling that my maturity date had more significance than the average Cloudarian. I am the queen's daughter and third in line for the throne. I kept my feelings to myself as not to spoil Themar's plans. She was true to her Thudanez' culture. They were fearless people who depended upon their king's expectations for their destiny. Since her king had not shared his expectations for her life, she could not give me a clue as to what to expect. "Hello! Anyone there?" Themar interrupted my internal thoughts. "Are you listening to me?" I asked her to repeat her last statement. She looked at me bewilderingly and repeated, "Have you decided to attend the Maturity Ball tomorrow for your birthday?" She reminded me that it was the first night I would be permitted to go out unaccompanied and without the security or my parents. She looked at me anxiously with her classic, unrelenting face, which she gave when she was serious. I decided to concede to her wishes, knowing that there wasn't any point in resisting her plans for me. I gave her a shy smile, and she got excited, knowing that she had won. "Have you decided on what you are going to wear to the ball?" Of course, this was an easy question for me; I didn't usually put much effort into what I wore. Usually, if I were to attend a special event, my clothing would be pre-selected for me as to leave no fashion mishap for the chance. My mother was a fashion icon, and she made sure that I did not embarrass myself or her. I had to admit, for the first time, I was excited to choose clothing for myself. Themar began to discuss styles that she thought would look attractive on me. I hoped she was joking! She knew that I had a simplistic approach as regards clothing, and she was a drama queen. When she noticed my expression, she stopped suggesting styles for my Maturity Ball. I had never been very good at hiding my thoughts. "Okay, what did you have in mind?"

she asked, with her hand on her hips. I put on a sheer baby blue long gown that hugged my slim hips and dipped low toward my lower back and flared my calves. When Themar saw me, she jumped up and hugged me. "I didn't know that you had it in you," she said. Whatever she meant ... I was just happy that she approved it, and it was one less thing we had to worry about before the ball. As we were rejoicing over my choice of gown for the ball, I received a script from my mother. "Honey, I do believe it's time for your training session with Bilow. You know how he gets when people are late... Signed, The Queen!" I wondered if she noticed that she signed her scripts "The Queen". I said to myself, "She is using her serious voice." I laughed to myself, knowing she was anything but serious. The queen was the life of the party and loved by all who knew her. Tamara must have speculated my mother's script. She hugged me and informed me that she would pick me up the next day, at sunset, for the Maturity Ball.

I entered Bilow's layer. As I expected, he was seated in his chair. He filled every inch of the massive chair with his tall frame with a contemplating look on his face. With his deep baritone voice, he said, "Airea, in addition to your traditional training, I need to speak with you. Please be seated." I quickly scurried to sit in front of him while wondering about his need to speak to me. He said, "I've had a complicated vision that involved you making an extremely important decisions that would change the course of our history." Hours later, I walked away from Bilow's layer, nauseous with fear of the future, asking myself what decisions I would be forced to make. I had not developed the potential capacity of my gift. Approximately five percent of our population had been blessed with unique gifts.

Suddenly, I felt ten years older with intoxicating thoughts of what was to come. I wondered for a while in a failed attempt to absolve my mind.

Once I finally arrived home, my mother was waiting for me with a somber expression. "Are you okay, honey? I spoke with Bilow when you didn't come home, and he told me about his vision. Don't worry; you know most visions can be interpreted," she said. This made me feel a little better even though she knew as well as I did that Bilow as the wisest interpreter in the history of Cloudarians. She attempted to change the subject by asking me if she could have a sneak peek at my gown. I smiled and shook my head, informing her once again that I wanted her to be surprised. I didn't think she was worried about my selection, but it was hard to tell. "You look tired, honey! You should turn in for the night," Mom said. I realized that my legs felt heavy, and I was not confident that I'd even make it to my chambers. Once in bed, I slept off and woke up in the middle of the night.

I had a recurring dream that I was on earth. There was a man that appeared to be my age, but I could not see his face. I yearned to see his face. I got up in a frenzy! When I realized that I slept longer than I intended, I sent a script to Themar. "I need help!!" Themar arrived with her down-to-the-business face, and I was not surprised that she was already dressed in a stunning gown with full makeup and hair. In a flash, she was spinning me around, putting skiver pins in my hair as she helped me accessorize my gown. I shifted into my gown.

The mad rush came to a halt. Tamara told me to look at myself. I couldn't believe my eyes. I looked at myself in the mirror, and I knew it was me, but I never knew I could look that beautiful. Themar adorned with my almond-shaped eyes with silver eye shadow, which accented the subtle blue hue in my translucent skin. Somehow, she gave me an illusion of full lips with a pink lip liner and gloss. She twisted my hair up with a few pieces, handing down at the nape of my neck and the base of my temples. For the first time, I felt like a woman. My mom walked into my chamber, as I had anticipated, and immediately started to cry. "You girls look absolutely breathtaking. Your father wished he could be here, but he had to attend a business meeting. Yet, he sends his love. You girls go and have fun, but be careful," Mom said as she looked in Themar's direction. Themar gave her a sheepish grin.

CHAPTER 2

The Night That Changed My Life

We arrived at Centennial Hall. I had dreamed of that day, and the reality of that night exceeded my dream. The event was colossal with a beautiful mural, elegant painting on the ceiling of the hall. The walls looked as if they were embedded with blue-tinted metal with specks of radiant diamonds. There was an assortment of blue, purple, and green flowers meticulously arranged at the center of each table, exuding the smell of lavender and gardenias. Themar's voice awakened my daze. She said, "Airea, isn't this amazing? Follow me!" She dragged me down a large staircase, and I was praying to The Core that I might not fall and royally embarrass myself. The host announced our arrival as Princess Airea Dorm and Lady Themar Lounce, and everyone stopped to bow. I could feel the blushing of my cheeks as I struggled to make myself comfortable with the unexpected attention. We were directed to our table. I noticed that our table had the most lavish design and was separated from the other tables. I said to myself: "I wish they had not done this!" As usual, Themar saw my disapproval and asked me if I would like to go to the dance floor. Our favorite artist was performing, so we went to the dance floor. They played a popular upbeat song to excite the crowd. Over the life cycles of the Cloudarian people, Cloudarians have assimilated many of the human cultures into their lifestyle, especially the younger generation. The older generation fought to hold sternly to the traditional values of the Cloudarian people. However, I appreciated both customs. They were both wonderful in their own ways.

Themar and I finally worked our way to the dance floor and danced. The band, Gerod, changed their tune to a slow, beautifully hauntingly melody. The lead singer softly whispered the melody, and everyone entered a trance-like state. Suddenly, I felt weird. It was as if someone was watching me. I nervously examined the room, and he was looking right at me. "Who is he? And why is he rudely staring at me?" He did not look much older than me with his hair as black as night and a sturdy, tall frame and forest green eyes. "Why is he staring at me so intently?" It was unsettling at the very least and completely inappropriate at best. His features were somehow imitating and inviting. He had a tall, strong, and agile body that command-ed respect. He was very tempting. His jet-black hair was thick and flowed back to the nape of his neck. His rich green eyes were so striking as if they pierced one's soul. The music induced a feeling of glee. Reluctantly, I was able to stop gazing at him. As I was dancing, I suddenly felt a light touch on my elbow. When I turned around, he was right behind me! Almost imme-diately, I had a nervous feeling in my stomach. It flipped, and I had a feeling I could not under-stand or articulate. I was sure of one thing: this boy was trouble. "May I cut in?" he said in vel-vet yet husky voice. Themar finally realized that the question was directed at her. She looked at me, intrigued and inquisitive. I felt he was try-ing to gauge my reaction. I reluctantly gave her a courteous nod. Themar left us at once with a polite nod. In a very formal and seductive tone, he said, "Good evening, Princess! My name is Prince Latherius, and I am very pleased to make your acquaintance." I gave him a quaint smile and said, "You can call me Airea!" I had never had the patience for my formal title. However, he respectfully insisted that he at least address me as Princess Airea. I gave him a quick nod since I was not sure what to say. I thought it might be a good idea to keep our interaction as formal as possible. My first impression was that the prince came from an elite linage. I was surprised that we hadn't run in the same circles. Suddenly, the song changed, and he placed his hand on my lower back and pulled me closer. He put my hand into his, and we continued dancing. I could tell that he liked to be in control, so I defied his request by pulling back to allow some space between our bodies. We swayed and twirled with the music until it stopped. He bade me farewell, saying, "Until next time!" as he gave me a youthful smile. In an instant, The-mar came bouncing up to me all giddy. She said, "Do you know who that was?" I told her he was some guy named Prince Latherius. She shook her head and told me the guy was Prince Lath-erius from her tribe, the Lidarian tribe. Before she could bombard me with several questions, I said to her, "I will give you the juice later." I was comforted to know that he was a Lidarian. Yet, I was still left with many questions. The rest of the night was magically filled with entertain-ment, dancing, and traditional rituals. Periodi-cally, I would catch him stealing quick stares at me. Gratefully, he did not approach me for the remainder of the night.

CHAPTER 3

My First Experience of Adulthood

The following morning, I woke up to a script from my mom, stating, "Good morning, dear! When you wake up, join your father and me at the table for breakfast." Upon arriving at the dining area, my mother and father were already seated. "Good morning, Princess! Sit down," my Father instructed. I took a seat, and Marenea brought my plate and beverage. She gave me a coy look and pranced away from the dining area. "So, tell me about your glandulous night without your old folks," my father said, with his usually playful smile. "Everything was wonderful. I had a wonderful time. It was pleasant to be on my own," I answered. "Surprisingly," he said, "you are an official Cloudarian adult. There is no shame in admitting that you want to be responsible and accountable for your actions. You are free to come and go as you please. We ask that you let us know where you are always and when to expect your return home. Additionally, you are expected to respect Tori's supervision. However, "The Eye" is looking over you at all times," my mom said. "Moms are always concern about their children's protection. I tend to forget about "The Eye," even though it has a view outside of the perimeters of my chambers. It feels like an intrusion of my privacy; however, I understand that it is for my safety. So, I know that there is no negotiating on this matter."

Dad interrupted my thoughts: "Well, it seems that you have made an impression on King Con's son, Prince Latherius. I received the first un-official script from King Con when we talked about a treaty several months ago. Do you know how many lives would be spared if you two were to wed?" Before I could catch myself, I spat out my beverage! "Marriage?" I almost screamed. My mother spoke, "What your father is trying to say... there is a lot at stake here if you two umm, hit it off?" My dad and I simultaneously burst into laughter at my mom's failed attempt to use contemporary terminology. She added, "Of course, if you don't think it will work between you two, there are no obligations." Somehow, a part of me knew it was not going to be that simple, and I started to get a little nauseous. I asked to be excused from the table. As soon as I got to my room, I sent Themar a script: "We need to talk." Once she arrived at my chambers, I shared my parent's conversation with her. For the first time in her life, she was speechless. After she gathered her thoughts, she asked, "What are you going to do?" I replied, "Honestly, I have no idea. I know, at least, I owe it to our people to meet with him and see what happens." "Well, at least he's hot," Themar squeaked, and we both laughed while nodding in agreement.

One day, I was to meet Prince Latherius. Between meeting the prince and anticipating my assignment from Bilow, it felt as if I was going to lose my breakfast. Every Cloudarian received an occupational assignment appointed by "The Core" and interpreted by none other than Bilow. I shared with Themar that the prince and I were to meet at some extravagant restaurant. It was one of the most upscale restaurants in our realm. Themar helped me to get dressed in a fitted, red silk dress. I loved the way the smooth material felt against my skin. I applied pink lipstick, and I felt like a woman. Themar assured me that I looked great, and I trusted her judgment.

I arrived at the restaurant, and a striking young woman wearing a Japanese inspired dress and a high tight hair bun was one of the hostesses. There are long rectangular fire pits inside every wall. The restaurant was elegant, comfortable, and cool. I spotted Latherius and walked up to his table. He stood up, pulled out the chair for me, and returned to his seat. He said, "I've already ordered. I hope you don't mind." I did mind, but I decided it was too early to pick a fight. I asked him, "What made you decide to ask me out for a date?" He seemed to ponder the question for a second before saying, "Honestly, I've been raised never to be afraid to go after something I want." Latherius' can-dor took me by surprise. I'd heard rumors about King Con. It was said that he was power-hungry and ruthless. Our tribes had engaged in count-less battles in the past due to his inability to adhere to our laws. However, I kept it to myself for the moment and changed the subject, "So what did you think about the ball?" "I thought it turned out better than I expected," he said, with one eyebrow cocked up. The waitress brought our food, and to my surprise, he ordered the most expensive items on the menu: flouting spouts and tangled leans. He must have antici-pated my thoughts. He told me that money was no object, and he would be greatly offended if I mentioned the cost. I looked on in bewilderment and mentally started listing the things I dis-liked about him. Halfway through our meal, he asked if I was nervous about which assignment I might receive. I automatically replied that I had full trust in The Core. He asked, "What if you had a choice? What would you choose to do with your life?" I said, "It has never occurred to me. I cannot imagine doing anything other than what I have been destined to do. This is how it's always been done," I replied. "I have heard of a rebellious group that plans to be the first to defy The Core's wisdom. Are you part of this group?" I asked him. For the first time, he looked shocked and then laughed out loud, which invited the attention and gaze of the other people in the restaurant. After he had contained his composure, he apologized, saying, "I am sorry. I am not accustomed to people who speak their minds around me. Of course, you know that is just a rumor." We finished our meal with a light conversation. However, I ended the night with more questions than answers.

As he walked me to my chambers, he looked as if he wanted to say something, but stopped himself. I must admit he had my pulse sprinting, wearing his sharp maroon suit. The glare from the moon made his jet-black hair shine as stars dotted in a majestic horizon. He looked at me, with his head slightly tilted to the side, and unconsciously licked his lips. He asked me to share my thoughts with him. I stuttered! Before I got a chance to answer, he quickly pulled me close to him and placed a firm hand on my bare lower back, and my legs almost gave out. As my body slumbered, he held me tightly. Not to reveal my reaction to his warm body, I whispered in his ear, "I wanted to see your black hair up close." His expression slightly changed, and he regrettably loosened his grip on me. He said, "People say that I look like my mother, but I wouldn't know. She died giving birth to me." Touched by that story, I wanted to hug him and ask him more about his mother, but I felt it was a touchy issue for him. He gave me a quick kiss on my cheek and said, "I would love to do this again. I had the most delightful evening." I snickered to myself and told him it would be a good idea. That said, I bade him goodnight. As soon as I entered my chambers, I sent a script to Themar, informing her that the evening went well and that I would share my experience with her as soon as possible. Having sent the script, I fell fast asleep.

CHAPTER 4

A Taste of Love

The following days, Prince Latherius sent me scripts, asking various questions about myself, such as my favorite color, food, and favorite childhood memory. This intrigued me. On the one hand, it seemed to be cute. Yet, I was not sure of his motives. My heart had butterflies, but my mind did not trust him. I did not know how, but somehow, he convinced me to go on a second date. The thought of a second date distracted me from my upcoming assignment with Bilow.

I immediately sent Themar a script. She came over to help me to prepare for my date with the Latherius. For some reason, Themar acted as if I was her doll. She immediately commanded me to shift into various outfits until she settled on a royal blue jumper with gold strapped high hills. She pinned half my hair up, and let the remainder fall down my back. She said, "The prince won't be able to keep his eyes off you in this ensemble." I gave her a girlish look, and we both laughed. Just as Themar left, Latherius showed up, looking handsome. He was dressed in a crisp white shirt, emerald green slacks with a casual messy hairstyle. I couldn't stop thinking to myself that he was gorgeous. As if he read my mind, he smirked and pulled me into a bear hug. I tried to resist him, but his intoxicating scent kept me locked in his arms.

For a moment, I inhaled and exhaled until I forced myself out of his trance. "Are you ready?"

he asked. I was afraid that my voice might break, so I nodded, and we took off. I followed him, unsure of our destination. After what seemed like an eternity of flying, we arrived at the edge of our realm, where the floggers usually entered the earth realm. They weren't jumping that day as each occupation was busy preparing for the ceremony the next day. Latherius said, "I have not been here since I was a child. I have forgotten how memorizing the portal can be. We are going on a picnic!" My only reference to a picnic was from my textbooks. He set up what appeared to be a lavish picnic. He looked so excited that it was contagious, and I smiled as he pulled out my chair for me and set my plate. Something was stirred inside me, and frankly, it scared me. "You are so beautiful," he said, as he squeezed my hand. Instantly, I felt a mild burning sensation that escalated my heart rate. "What are you afraid of?" In reply, I asked him,

"Who says I'm afraid of anything?" He seemed to contemplate whether to pursue this line of questioning. I guessed he decided against it and asked, "What do you think about me?" I didn't like the question because I was not sure of the truth value of what I knew about him. So, I said, "I like that you make me laugh, and I like being around you." Then I talked to myself, "Wow! I just told a boy that I liked being around him." It was the first time that I ever said such words to a boy. He looked like he was flabbergasted, not knowing what to say. "I have noticed you do that a lot." He asked, "I do what?" "Second guess yourself," I retorted. He cocked an eyebrow and said, "That's how I was raised." I said to myself, "If his father is as strict as people say, it makes sense that he should second guess himself." Yet, I was not sure about my thoughts because neither one of us had spoken about our parents. It seemed to be an unspoken rule that we do not to talk about our parents. We talked about how we felt about the Cloudarian ceremony. He said that I was so lucky that my maturity date was so close to the annual Cloudarian assignment ceremony.

We started to walk along the edge of the portal, then I paused. Latherius turned to me and put his hand at the nape of my neck. He began to play with pieces of my hanging hair, and my breathing went into overdrive. He looked deeply into my eyes as if he saw my thoughts and kissed me lightly on the corner of my mouth. Without hesitation, he pulled me into a kiss with so much depth that I thought I was going to pass out. We pulled away at the same time. Both of us panted and gasped for air. He looked at me with his green eyes, and I could hear my heartbeat in my ears. Once we calmed down, we made our way back to my chambers. When we arrived, I tried to say a quick goodbye, but he pulled me into a hug and laced his fingers into mine. He kissed me on my cheek and wished me the best for the assignment the following day. He jetted off at lightning speed. Entering my chambers, Themar was already waiting for me. She jumped on me with a speculator's eyes. I told her everything without leaving out any details. I blushed when I told her about the kisses, and she squealed with delight. "So, does that mean that you two are officially dating?" Themar asked. "I do not know what we are doing or if I want us to be doing anything," I said.

Themar decided to spend the night with me. We watched Catch-up on the Hilo series. My parents wished us the best of the ceremony the next day, and I could tell they were more excited than we were about our assignments.

CHAPTER 5

A Ceremony of Life's Assignment

---

*M*y alarm chimed, signaling we had forty-five minutes to leave. My parents sent a script that they had already left and to be sure that we were not late for the ceremony. We quickly shifted into the customary outfits and hastily made our way to the hallow grounds, where everything was to take place. On arrival, we were given a number each and told to get into line. Bilow's voice permeated over all the noise, and instantaneously, all the chatter dissipated. Bilow welcomed everyone, and we began our customary chant to The Core. We were instructed to enter the lake of life one at a time. The lake was located at the center of coliseum. It was bright blue with blue mist floating from its surface. The first person to enter was a girl I didn't recognize. She seemed to be fearful of entering the water.

There had always been a rumor that The Core lived at the bottom of the lake. I felt bad for her, knowing it had to be scaring being the first one to enter the lake. She seemed to gain her courage and entered the water with an audible gasp. She treaded forward to Bilow, who placed an unknown device on his index fingers. He placed it on her temple and announced that she would be a star keeper. The crowd applauded and cheered. One by one, the line moved forward, and Latherius entered the lake. Bilow placed his index fingers on Latherius's temple and announced he was to be a judge. I took a deep breath as he entered the water. I thought Themar noticed my reaction because I could see her shoulders bouncing as she was laughing. After what seemed to be a lifetime of waiting, it was Themar's turn. She was also appointed to be a judge. The people gasped! It was uncommon to have two judges appointed in the same ceremony. Finally, it was my turn, and my heartbeat rapidly increased. I had assumed the water would be cold, but instead, it was refreshing. It was replenishing to the body. I could tell Bilow had to struggle to keep his expression under control. He brought his finger to my temple, and it felt like electric currents flowing through my body. I didn't know if it was the effect of the electrical currents, but it seemed like it took longer for him to announce my assignment. Finally, he said, "You will be a flogger!" Everyone shouted and applauded.

Floggers were assigned once everyone thousand years. I was in a daze until the end of the ceremony. Once the ceremony ended, Themar and I met our parents at the Owl. The Owl was a historic restaurant where people with power dined. After our parents toasted and congratulated us, they informed us of where we were to report for additional instructions. I could not believe that our training would start that soon. Our eyes locked onto Latherius and his parents as they entered the restaurant and sat at the opposite end of the restaurant. Latherius had a direct view of me. I do not know if it was intentional, but it seemed as if everything he did was directed at me.

I was squirming in my seat, and Themar nudged me with her elbow. I excused myself and went to the restroom to gather my composure. As I was leaving the restroom, Latherius grabbed my elbow and spun me around into a secluded corner. He didn't say anything. He just looked at me with his suggestive, green eyes. After a moment of silence, he said, "I haven't been able to stop thinking about you. What have you done to me?" I said, "Nothing!" I knew that his question was rhetorical. He said, "I want to congratulate you on your assignment. I'm happy with my assignment, but I wish I could be with you." I said, "Honestly, I'm a little afraid to go." "You will be fine," he said, as his palm caressed my cheek. He released me, and we walked our separate ways. I rejoined my family, and he didn't look at me again for the remainder of the evening.

CHAPTER 6

Crunch Time

The next day, I reported to the location indicated on my form at 6:00 am sharp. My instructor was a short curly-headed Tunkaz male. I could tell right away that he was Tunkaz because they all had curly hair that looked windblown. However, I was surprised that a Tunkaz was a flogger since they were usually assigned to monitor natural disasters. He said, "My name is Sargent Harie Pouple, but you may call me Harie." He was clearly an older man, but he had a youthful appearance. I could tell that we were going to become good friends. He said to me, "The first quarter, we will study the history of the floggers. You will be tested at the end of the quarter. In the second quarter, you will be trained to dive with simulated dive equipment. In the last week of the second quarter, you will have a supervised dive to earth. If you pass your tests and training, you will be an official flogger. Take a seat, and we will begin our lessons."

Harie taught me the fundamentals of flogging:

Floggers are the only ones that get a chance to go through the portal to the human realm. Floggers study human science, art, history, and psychology. The study of these disciplines helps our people to keep up with human culture. The older generation of Cloudarians has no interest in the new-age pop culture of humans. They are only interested in their scientific achievements.

My studies were strenuous, and I barely had time to socialize. Themar said her training was also stressful. She complained that she had so much to learn in a short time. She complained about having to share classes with Latherius. However, she was thrilled that she had an opportunity to keep a close eye on him. I laughed, knowing that she was not kidding. "I'm also keeping an eye on our instructor. I think Judge Prima may be a cougar and has a thing for your man," Themar said. In a panic, I almost choked on my saliva with an emotional spasm that I couldn't express.

The next morning, I received a script from Latherius. His image popped up in the middle of my room, and I almost forgot how handsome he was. It looked as if he had just taken a shower because his hair was wet. "Good morning, Airea! I apologize that so much time has passed since I've spoken to you. I want to assure you that

I've thought of you. My training has consumed more time than expected. I hope all is well with you, and I hope to see you once my training has ended." I changed into a pale pink dress and ran my hands through my hair. I sent him a quick message: "Hi, Latherius! No apologies are necessary. I completely understand, and I need to get ready before I'm late for my training. Today, we're learning how human pollution has affected our weather patterns. I have missed you as well."

After a sundry of weeks, we took our final exams, and our training ended. True to our tradition, we made plans to celebrate at the Hub. I met Themar at her chambers to catch up and get ready for the celebration. As expected, we took the time to advise each other on wardrobe choices.

Afterward, we went to the Hub, though we were late! Entering the Hub, Latherius flagged us to join his table. Getting close to his table, Latherius eyed me appreciatively and swiftly got to his feet and pulled out my chair. His shivery wasn't lost on me. Themar quickly got to her seat before he even thought about doing the same for her. He introduced me to his guest, and we made small talk. Judge Prima sat next Latherius. It gave me a funny vibe. From our conversation, I learned that she had been a judge's instructor for five hundred years. I was shocked that she looked so young. Themar told me something about her, but she didn't tell me that she was drop-dead gorgeous. I wondered if she thought I was jealous of her working so close to Latherius. As she was reading my mind, Themar playfully nudged me. Other than the occasional side glances from Prima, the rest of the night went without a hitch. We all said our goodbyes. I realized that I had left my pocket halo at the table.

Love and Illness

I returned to our table to get my halo from the deserted table. As I walked back toward the door, I felt a firm hand grabbing my wrist. Latherius pulled me into a darkened hallway. I could hear my heart pounding in my ears as I heard a scream of terror forming in the back of my throat. Before the scream escaped, the terror was replaced by a burning heat as Latherius' lips hungrily met mine. He must have felt my knees trembling because he placed his other hand firmly on my lower back. He exhaled a deep breath as if he had been holding it all night. "What are you doing to me?" he asked. I just looked at him because I didn't know what to say. He stroked his index and middle finger along my cheek and slowly down my neck, leaving a fiery path everywhere his hand touched me. My breath hitched! I was breathless with an uncontrollable feeling that would have surely consumed me if he hadn't stopped.

"Please!!!" I pleaded. Mercifully, he understood my plea and stopped but left his hand on my lower back to hold me as I tried to get my composure. I took a few deep breaths, but that only made matters worse because I inhaled his intoxicating scent. He said, "I didn't get a chance to tell you how breathtaking you look tonight." I responded, "So you decided to take my breath away." Simultaneously, we burst out in laughter, which got the attention of the other guests. He said, "I think we should go before this love volcano erupts."

We made it back to my chambers and sat outside in the garden. I decided to ask the question. "So, what's the deal between you and Prima?" He looked perplexed. "There is not a "deal" between us, but she has expressed interest in romance. I graciously declined her advance, and we have maintained a professional relationship. Look, Airea! I have never had a romantic interest in anyone before you, and it certainly has nothing to do with forming a truce with your people. If our relationship produces peace among our people, it is just a bonus." I realized that I was holding my breath, and I had to remind myself to breathe. "Thanks for your honesty, but I do need you to promise me something tonight." "Anything!" he said. "I want you to promise me if things do not work out between us, that we will always remain friends," I told him. He pondered for a while and said, "I promise to honor your decision, but it will be challenging to be just friends." We sat comfortably at the moment, meditating upon his answer. He gently and slowly turned my face to his face and meticulously fixed his lips upon my lips. He said to me, "You are the most beautiful creature that I have ever had the pleasure of observing." I didn't know how to respond to his statement of affection. I just squirmed in my seat. He smiled with his crooked smile, seemingly satisfied with my reaction. I was frightened and thrilled that he had control over my sexual impulse. If I could, I would curse myself. So, he said to me, "When do you go through the portal?" I said, "In two weeks, and I have no earthly idea of how it is going to feel." "They tried explaining the effects of the portal upon our body, but I guess it's just something I must experience. Well, we have two free weeks to do what we want until we report for official duties," he responded. I smiled but said nothing. Suddenly, I felt lethargic. He must have noticed this because he kissed me goodnight.

The next day, I was supposed to meet with Latherius, but I had to cancel. My mom summoned the family physician. I told her not to do it that I was just feeling a little strange, possibly due to the lack of sleep. I gave up, knowing that was no use. It's not that I didn't like Doctor Taron; it's just that doctors crept me out altogether. Doctor Taron entered my room, looking older than I remembered. "Hello, Airea! You sure have grown up to be a stunning young lady. What seems to be ailing you, my child?" asked Dr. Taron. I told him about feeling unnerving energy that felt like it was charging within my body. "It started yesterday, but it feels as if the current is growing stronger," I concluded. Doctor Taron scanned my body. He looked over the results and determined that other than a slightly elevated heart rate, everything was fine. Before he left, he turned to me and suggested that maybe I could be suffering from anxiety from all the "changes" that had occurred in my life. There was a sigh of relief from my parents, but something inside of me knew that anxiety was not the answer. Before I could worry myself any further, my vision began to blur, and the last thought was that I must have been given a sedative.

I began to dream. It started at the same place as if it was on replay. I jumped through the portal and came out through a murky fog. There he was! Working in what looked like some sort of field, he took my breath away. I could not breathe. I really could not breathe.

I woke up, gasping for air. I looked at the clock and rubbed my eyes to be sure I saw the date correctly. I had slept for two days. "How do you feel?" my mother asked in a concerned tone. Her hair was disheveled, and I wondered how long she had been in my room. I felt okay! Honestly, I hadn't had a chance to assess how I felt. "The doctor said you were suffering from exhaustion and anxiety. Bilow heard of your condition and was here yesterday to see you. He has determined that you need rest. I have many messages from your friends asking about you. Should I send a group message, informing them that you are feeling well?" "That would be great. Thanks!" I said. I drank Marenea's special concoction, which she prepared for me when I was ill. It tasted awful, but it always seemed to help. I would not dare ask her for the ingredients.

I sent Themar a script, and she accepted it. Her face popped up. Before I could speak a word, she was already scolding me for not contacting her with an update on my health. I informed her that after speaking to my mother, she was the first call I made, and she was pacified. "Are you nervous about the portal jump? We have less than twelve days before we start our assignments," Themar said. "Well, if I wasn't worried before, I sure am now. I think I need another sedative!" I retorted. She burst into laughter. We wished each other good luck and said our goodbyes.

I realized after we hung up that I had no earthly idea of what I needed to wear for my jump. After some time, I decided to wear a flattering version of my combat training attire. I looked at the clock, and I was not satisfied to see I had wasted two hours. I decided to go for a walk in the garden to calm my nerves. I heard a rustling noise, and Bilow appeared, frightening me. "Sorry, I hope I did not scare you, my child," he said. "I had to see for myself that all was well. Also, I'm afraid to say that your parents' wishes may not be your destiny. Your heart will wage war. Whatever you decide will be the right decision. However, your decision will have grave consequences. When the time comes for you to make the most critical decision of your life, everyone in your life will have an opinion. You are to listen to your heart. I don't wish to burden you, but it is imperative that you don't let anyone sway your decisions. If you make the wrong decision, there will be irreversible repercussions. The Core knew what it was doing when it chose your destiny." In a flash, Bilow was gone. I searched for him everywhere. He was gone. I knew he was there, but I wondered if I was suffering from the effects of the sedative. So, I decided to turn in for the evening.

CHAPTER 8

The Ecstasies of Earth

The day of the day finally came. Due to my illness, Latherius and I did not get a chance to have our moments of love before our assignments. My alarm sounded, and I jumped up out of bed, all excited and nervous. I rushed and got dressed. I decided it was best to skip breakfast, so I bade my parents farewell. I headed for the portal and made it there in record time. Sargent Harie was already in the air-tracker accompanied by a young man dressed in flogger gear. The young man appeared to be my age. As I stood in front of them, Harie introduced him as Whiley. He shook my hand enthusiastically, with a wide grin. I didn't know why, but I had a feeling that we were going to become good friends. I was aware that I would have to co-jump but wasn't sure of who it would be. At least, some fears would be put to rest. Harie stated the jump protocol as if he had been through it numerous times. Having reviewed the information so many times during my training, I could articulate it verbatim. Once Harie was satisfied that we were ready to jump, we joined hands, and Harie input the directions into air-trackers.

Simultaneously, Whiley and I stepped through the portal. As soon as we stepped through the portal, time sprang us downward at warp speed. I couldn't feel my body, but I could hear muffled sounds. Just when I felt like

I was going to lose consciousness, everything stopped, and I opened my eyes, gasping for air. Mentally, I could see Hari yelling something, but I couldn't comprehend. All I could do was try to remember how to breathe. Finally, my training kicked in, and I was able to calm myself by clearing my mind. My rapid breathing slowed down to a normal rhythm.

I saw my surroundings for the first time. It was the daytime. It seemed like we were in some sort of wheat field. I'd never seen wheat before, but I remembered the pictures of it. I slowly brushed my hand along the tips of the grains. A giggle escaped my mouth because it tickled my hand, and I couldn't help myself. I ran through the field, soaking in the sun. Whiley ran after me, but I didn't care. I reveled the feel of the ground underneath my feet. Even though we could walk and run in Cloudarian, gravity is different. "I can't describe the feeling. I must slow my stride because my limbs feel shaky. I must sit before I fall. Whiley flops down beside me with a look of amusement. After some time, he speaks, 'How does it feel to you?' 'It's a little overwhelming,' I say. 'Are you ready to meet our keeper?' he asks. 'I'm as ready as I'll ever be,' I affirm. Then our trackers join us in the field, we follow them through the field, up a steep hill, and across a small creek and to a house enclosed by a white fence."

I accessed my architectural data, and I believed it was a ranch style home with dark oak panels and green shutters. I must admit that the house looked very cozy and inviting. Suddenly, the door opened, and it was an older woman with long black hair. "Hello! My name is Daisy," she said. "Come in! Come in! Make yourself at home!" she said, and we entered the house. We took a seat in a room that had a table and chairs. "You two get comfortable, and I'll get you some sweet tea and cucumber sandwiches," Daisy said and left. She returned, bearing with a platter of sandwiches, sweet tea, and fruits. Then she placed a vase with a purple flower on the table. According to my studies, the flowers appeared to be hydrangeas. Daisy set our dishes in front of us, and for the first time, I heard my stomach make a weird rumbling sound, and I jumped. Whiley burst into laughter at my reaction, and I felt my cheeks blush with embarrassment. Daisy gave him a stern look. He quickly contained himself and informed me that I was experiencing hunger. Cloudarians eat but not to satisfy hunger. As we ate, we made small talks. Daisy gave us some brief house rules. She informed us that her nephew would arrive in the morning, and he would be staying with her over the summer for the college break. Whiley had a concerned look on his face. As if she read his mind, she added that her nephew was soon to be a keeper, as he was in training. Afterward, she showed us to our living quarters.

The next day, I woke up to the sound of sizzling and a delectable aroma. I hurriedly got dressed and headed downstairs. Daisy made her specialty: peach pancakes and cheese grits. She said, "I make the best coffee you'll ever taste." "I think I have found my favorite human food!" I said to myself. Knowing that Cloudarians are what humans consider vegetarians, she knew not to prepare meats for us. I ate until we could eat no more. Whiley and I said our goodbyes. He was to return in four weeks to bring me back home. Whiley received the necessary data for our official assignment. Every flogger, on their first jump, remained on earth for one month. The compilation data prepared floggers for future short jumps.

Sitting on the porch, I saw a silver pickup truck with a streak of red kicking up dust while pulling up to the house. "I hope that this is the nephew. I'm not sure that I'm ready to meet a normal human," I contemplated. However, I made sure that my posture was receptive. As the vehicle got closer, I felt anxiety building up in my stomach. The truck came to an abrupt stop, the door swung open, and he stepped out. I choked on my own saliva! He ran up to me and patted me hard on the back. I felt somewhat embarrassed. Once I regained my composure, we made our introductions and shook hands. He told me that his name was Hunter. As soon as our hands touched, I felt a surge of electricity run through me, and everything went black.

When I opened my eyes, I was gazing at the ceiling fan in my quarters. "How did I get to my bed?" I asked. Daisy answered, "You passed out!" She frightened me! I did not realize that she was sitting in a chair in the corner of my room. I slowly sat up, but my head was swimming. Daisy gave me warm tea, mixed with herbs. As I drank it, I began to feel better. I lay back down and woke up later that night. Daisy warmed up my dinner and informed me that it was past her bedtime. I finished my dinner, and he walked into the room with his disheveled golden hair. "Hey! There are you! Feeling okay?" he said as he grabbed a snack. He joined me at the table, turning the chair backward as to straddle it. "So, Daisy told me that you would spend your summer with her," he asked. "Yes, that's correct, and I cherish every moment," I answered. "Tennessee is a beautiful state and has many wonderful sites, especially Gatlinburg. We are in a small town called Townsend. It has a population of 448," he explained. We sat for a while, as he shared general information about Tennessee. I didn't mention that I already knew about Tennessee because I didn't want to be perceived rude. My training dwelled on Tennessee culture.

A yawn escaped as if to alert me that it was time to sleep. He reminded me of the house rule. Gracefully, I quickly rinsed and placed my dishes in the weird contraption called a dish-washer, as I was shown how to utilize earlier. We said goodnight and went our separate ways. I slipped into a satin short set nightgown and snuggled underneath the comforter. The win-dow was slightly cracked, and I could hear night creatures. My brain instantaneously detected the source of each sound. The crickets, frogs, and various insects formed a lullaby choir, and before I knew it, I drifted into a deep sleep.

"What! Huh!" I awoke to Hunter, shaking my shoulders. "Sorry, I don't mean to laugh, but you must have been having one interesting dream. I could hear you across the hall," Hunter said. I was terrified of what I might have said, so I decided not to ask. An uncomfortable silence passed over us. He nervously ran his hand through his thick curly hair. I was amazed that it bounced back perfectly. "Daisy was going to wait another day before putting you to work. However, since you're already up, I could show you the ropes," Hunter said. I was actually about to head out, so I did not want to, but before I could stop myself, I nodded my head in agreement. "You may want to grab a sweater. I'll meet you at the back door with your boots," Hunter advised. I grabbed a sweater, and I was not sure why, but for some reason, I felt the need to check myself out in my mirror. I hastily brushed my hair into a loose ponytail and applied some pink lip gloss. Even though dressing up was much faster, I kind of liked the feel of having to fix myself up. I was not sure Themar would appreciate it as much as I did since she shifted into a new look three to four times a day. She said her look must always fit her mood. I quickly left my chambers with a feeling of homesickness.

Once I met up with Hunter, he handed me the boots. He instructed me to keep my voice low and calm so that I wouldn't startle the horses. As soon as I entered the barn, I stumbled over a large rock embedded into the ground. Before I could stop myself, I yelled out, as a sharp pain radiated up my ankle, and I stumbled to the ground. The horses instantly started to buck in distress. Hunter cursed to himself and quickly ran to my side, asking me repeatedly if I was okay. "No, I'm not okay!" I said sharper than intended. "Sorry, I think I just sprained my ankle. Even though I know I will heal before the sun rises, I fear I may need something for this pain," I said, still in pain. The horses began to settle down as he pulled a red box, with a white cross on it, off one of the dusty shelves. Fumbling, he pulled something that looked like a wrapping out of a box. He said, "This is a first aid kit…" "And that is gauze!" I finished his sentence. Slightly annoyed, he seemed to forget that I had a vast knowledge of earth and its manufactured goods. The flogger who jumped five years ago updated our data bank.

"Can I see your ankle?" he requested. I slowly stretched my leg toward him, anticipating pain. However, the pain had subsided. He removed my boot and slowly doffed my sock. As soon as he gripped my ankle, a gasp of air escaped my lips. I could feel a vibration reverberating throughout my body. He instantly let go. He removed his hands from my ankle, believing that he had hurt me. "I'm so sorry. I didn't mean to hurt you," he apologized. "You didn't hurt me," I whispered. Looking perplexed, he slowly gasped and placed his hands on my ankle. He rubbed it with a pain ointment, and I felt a relaxing heat radiating through my body. I wondered if the ointment was the cause for the elevation of my body temperature. Then I said to him, "I feel better." I was desperate for him to unleash my ankle. "Okay, stand and try to put weight on it," he instructed. I stood, and to my surprise, a dull ache had replaced the sharp pain. "All good!" I said with a shy smile. I didn't know why I suddenly felt passionate about Hunter. I had never felt that way before, not even with Latherius.

Unfortunately, I had no one to talk to who could help me analyze my feeling. I missed Themar more than ever. "Earth to Airea!" Hunger's voice snapped me out of my thoughts. "Sorry! What did you say?" I asked him. "I asked if you would want to head back for the house," Hunter replied. "No, I can help! I'm fine!" I assured him. We made small talks while we tended to the horses. I explained to him that in our realm, we could fly short distances; otherwise, we had flying vessels. "We don't have to eat because we get our energy from "The Core". When we do eat, we take vegetarian diets," I explained to him. "I'm sorry," he remarked. "No need to be sorry! You can't miss what you've never had," I responded. "That's because you've never had fried chicken!" he said, with a huge smile on his face. He showed me how to brush the horses. He placed the brush in my hand and positioned his hand over mine. He was talking to me, but all I could hear was muted noise and electricity and heat surging through my body. My knees almost buckled, but I summoned all my strength and regained my balance. I could feel the electricity fading, and I snapped back to reality. I was relieved that I was able to control my reaction to Hunter's touch. Now I needed to figure out why I had the reactions.

For the rest of the week, I tried to limit contact with Hunter. By the end of the week, I began to run out of excuses. I feared that he would catch on to the fact that I'd been avoiding him. The truth was that I just needed time to analyze my feelings and try to focus on my duties. Feeling gratified that I'd caught up on my research, I went into the kitchen and found Daisy cleaning. "Airea, would you like to go to town to shop for a dress?" Daisy asked me. I tried to hide my excitement. "Um, sure! I'm happy to shop, but why do I need a dress?" I asked her. "Have you forgotten the Counsel Gala? Since you are here during the annual

Gala, you are expected to attend. It would be a great sign of disrespect if you did not attend. And since you are protector, your secrets with our people might be exposed," she explained. I apologized, explaining that it slipped my mind. Daisy put on her makeup and said, "We'll be ready to leave in thirty minutes."

We arrived in town. According to my studies and recalls of photos, we were at an outside mall. I was relieved that it wasn't a densely populated mall, and my nerves were calmed. I retrieved my human training and recalled my training on human disposition and body language. Daisy looked at me with a look of concern, but she was patient. I opened the door with confidence, excitement, and regret that my friend was not there with me. The shopping thing was some-what new to me. However, Themar would always help me get ready for any big event we had to attend. I refocused, knowing that Themar would want me to enjoy myself. Daisy and I agreed to go in different directions as we shopped and to meet back at the changing rooms in thirty minutes. She handed me a phone and looked at me, sternly. "If you have any problems, no matter how minor they are, call me. This is a new experience for you, and I don't want you to be embarrassed. If you are unsure about how things work here, call me!" she said and pointed me to changing rooms before she left. Knowing that it was going to be a formal event, I went to the gowns section. I picked dresses that I thought Themar would approve and that was also comfortable to me. "Ha, Themar isn't here to make me push my limits, and I blend into the crowd for once," I said to myself. Thirty minutes later, we met up at the dressing rooms and started to try on the gowns. A few times, I had to get Daisy's or the attendant's assistance to figure out how to put on a dress. Some of the dresses had straps that were confusing to me. It was so embarrassing. We agreed on a long-fitted dress for Daisy. She looked amazing, especially for her age, which I guessed was in the early fifties. She was tall and slim, unlike my human form. I guess you could call me slim; however, I seemed to have a 'curvy" body while on earth. I had not noticed my body shape until the. As if sensing my frustration, Daisy slung a dress over my door. My jaw dropped! I was surprised that she picked out such a sexy dress for me. She said, "You only live once. Just try it and see what you think!" I put the dress on, and without looking in the mirror in my dressing room, I walked out. The salesclerk looked at me and blurted out: "You look hot!" I looked at myself in a full-length mirror, and I had to agree with the salesclerk. The dress fitted me as if it was made for me. It had a scoop neck with delicate straps that wrapped around my neck and a plunging low back that showed off my shape in a flattering way. The deep pink material was the most unusual. It reminded me of the material that the Egyptians wrapped their mummies, and a giggle escaped me. Daisy's eyebrows furrowed, "Do you not like the dress? I think you look amazing," she said. Unsure why I couldn't stop laughing, I caught my breath and told her why I was laughing. She laughed and told me that I looked like one sexy mummy. I didn't know why, but I was grateful for the moment. I felt like I had begun to transition from me being her guest to becoming her friend. We got our accessories and checked out. It was a full girl's day: hair salon, manicure, and pedicure. I was exhausted. We decided to pick up fast food. Daisy told me that Hunter would more than likely be back that night after visiting with friends for the previous two days. I hated to admit that the news excited me. I was not sure why. I did let myself admit that I had feelings for him other than friends.

It was the day of the Gala, and my body was buzzing with nervous energy. The other night, Daisy dropped a bomb on me, stating it was customary to be escorted to the Ball. She said, "Hunter had volunteered." I felt obligated to say yes, after all the things that Daisy had done for me. She stated that she could get a higher-ranking guardian to escort me, but it would be her honor for her nephew to escort me. How could I say no? She told me that Hunter had completed his guardian apprenticeship and was a guardian. "So, you are telling me he has known my identity all this time?" I said more sharply than I had intended. "Please do not upset me! We are sworn to secrecy from everyone, including you, until my training is completed," she said.

Once I realized that she was just finding out as well, my heart rate slowed. "It's getting late. We should wash up and start getting ready for the gala," she said. "If you need help with your hair, let me know," she added. "I'm afraid I will, thank you!" I replied. After we got all dolled up, we went downstairs to meet the guys.

As soon as we went down the stairs, John let out a low whistle. "You ladies look amazing!" he said in his charming southern drawl. They escorted us to John's Black F150. It was so high off the ground that they had to give us a boost. We made small talks on the way to the gala. Daisy gave me an idea as to what to expect. They had a ceremony before dinner. Hunter gave me a gentle squeeze of assurance. It was a sweet gesture. However, I could feel my body heat elevating, moving up my neck, and my cheek blushing.

We turned off the main road to an unkempt dusty path into the woods. Finally, after three miles, a paved road appeared. A gate appeared from nowhere; we gained entrance and parked in a large parking garage, which overlooked a magnificent mansion. It had a pearly white color that almost sparkled. It shocked me. I was unaware that human architecture was that advanced. It was very modern and had a futuristic look. As if reading my mind, John said, "The last flogger to visit us had a knack for architecture. He helped us design this place with some help from your leaders as a gift." As I entered the main hall, it took my breath away. Rainforest was the theme of the year. They truly outdid themselves! The scent of intoxicating flowers and foliage was refreshing and relaxing. As we were escorted to our table, brief introductions were made. The fog on the floor reminded me of home.

Once seated at our table, our drinks and appetizers were brought to us. Hunter whispered in my ear, "I'm not sure I'm capable of behaving myself while you are wearing that dress. You take my breath away." I was not sure what to say, so I simply replied with a smile. He looked at me as if he wanted to say something, but he was interrupted by a tap on the microphone. A very unusually tall man tapped on the microphone to get our attention. "Good evening, everyone," he said with an odd accent. His olive skin was slightly aged. He had black hair with a large streak at each temple and almond-shaped brown eyes. He continued, "We want to welcome you to our annual Gala. I'm so delighted to see each one of you." He had a pointed look at me. Unsure why he looked at me, I squirmed under his gaze. He went on: "The purpose of this Gala is to assure our bond is secure and to orient our recruits. Please, may all the recruits stand?"

Looking proud, Hunter smiled with a quick wink at me. We ate our dinner, and I was glad that the ceremony wasn't too long.

After the ceremony, a live band began to play. It was an all-girl rock band, and they were surprisingly good. I'd never heard the beat or melody of the music. It was electrifying. Hunter stood and held out his hand toward me and led me to the dance floor. Gratefully, the fog had risen to provide some privacy. I felt a little self-conscious. It seemed as if everyone's eyes were on me. Hunter began to dance. I decided to push my anxiety away and enjoy the moment. I allowed myself to flow with the methodic rhythm. We swayed together to the beat of the drums. I could feel a magnetic pulse as our bodies got entangled in dance. He had to feel it! His head slowly fell backward. Even though I couldn't hear over the music, I felt a cool exhaling of his breath from his lips as he pulled me closer to him. He did it gently and seductively that it intensified our raw energy. It felt like my body was experiencing a heated massage. Reluctantly, I pulled away. Even though I felt an urge to stay in the moment, I felt compelled to go to the nearest powder room. I pointed to the ladies' room. I pulled Hunter down to me to whisper in his ear that I would meet him at the bar. I instantly regretted pulling him so close because a need to kiss him became nearly irresistible. Almost jogging, I headed for the ladies' room. As soon as I entered, something covered my mouth. I heard a click indicating the door had been locked, and my heart skipped a beat.

I attempted to calm my nerves by tapping into my training, and then I heard a soft voice saying, "Please, everything is okay. It's me!" Instantly, I recognized the voice, but how could it be? I removed my hand from my mouth, and I slowly turned: "Themar!" I squeaked out. "Yes, it's me," she said. "I miss you!" I said. "I miss you, but unfortunately, I can't stay long. My hologram will disappear in a few minutes. Bilow won't be able to maintain our connection for much longer," Themar said. As we spoke, his energy began to fade, and my connection weakened.

Themar quickly explained why Bilow sent her.

Bilow had a vision that Latherius and Hunter orchestrated a coup. The Lidarians and other tribal leaders intend to eliminate humankind and take control of earth and our realm. Your new mission is to find out why, and most importantly, how they plan to achieve this goal. Hunter has brainwashed Daisy. To break the spell, have Daisy to repeat these words: 'tumeish-youzerith.' It will break the spell and protect her from future attacks. Once the spell is broken, she can be trusted and can help you to achieve your mission. Your mission will require a strategy utilizing unconventional methods. Also, Hunter has been brainwashed. However, Bilow is unable to retrieve the information to release his mind from the spell. He was able to see two possible outcomes. The first outcome is that you will be able to release his mind from the spell and figure out their plans. The second outcome is that you will need to kill Hunter. If you fail, their plan will be successful, and you will not be able to prove their conspiracy. Regarding the electric sensation you've been feeling, use it too!

Themar's voice became muffled, and her image began to flicker, and she was gone. There was so much I wanted to say to Themar and so many unanswered questions. Knowing that I had already taken too long with Themar, I knew that Hunter would begin to either become suspicious or start worrying about me. Grateful for my training on controlling high stress, I repeated the mantra and took a deep breath. I saw Hunter at the bar looking at his watch. I quickly walked toward him. He asked me if I was okay as he ran his hand through his thick hair, and it fell back into place. "Um no, I think I must have eaten something bad. I'm not feeling well," I said. Hunter took control. We said our goodbyes to some of the other guests. Thankfully, a couple that lived nearby offered to take us home in their jeep. Daisy and John stayed at the Gala. Cursing myself for not thinking this plan through, I unintentionally planned to be alone with Hunter until Daisy returned to the house. I got control of my nerves by focusing on my strength and combat training. Even in my human form, I was stronger than any human. I could only be defeated while sleeping or intentionally letting my guard down. Since I didn't plan on letting down my guard, and I would sleep with a force-field around my room, I relaxed. For a while, we rode in silence. And for once, I was grateful. "So, it's my turn to ask a question," Hunter says. His voice snapped me out of my trance. "Umm, okay...!" I said. "What is that electric charge all about? I've been around your kind before, but I never felt it," he asked. Answering his question with a question, I asked him: "When have you been around "my kind"? The last flogger was sent to Japan." In a sharp tone, he said, "I met Turin. The man who helped build the palace we just left, remember? You didn't answer my question!" he reiterated. Irritated, I said: "I can't answer your question since I have no clue what's it's about. I hadn't experienced it until recently, and I haven't had time to ask an elder." Seemingly satisfied with my answer, he dropped it.

When we arrived at Daisy's house, he invited me to sit with him at the lake. Wanting to know more about him and needing to break his spell, I accepted. As we sat in a swinger, I wrapped my arm around him. The night was pleasantly warm with a light breeze. The moon glowed with magnificent hues of purple, gold, and pink. We sat in silence for a moment. He broke the silence by asking if I felt okay. I just nodded my head. My throat was thick with tension. "I was just wondering if you feel what I feel. It's like I need to tell you things, but something is holding me back. It is killing me to hold back what I feel," I said to him. Not even thinking, my body overrode my mind, and I drew him to me and gave him an earth-shuddering kiss. He responded by kissing me softly and passionately as if his life depended on it. To my surprise, the kissing broke the spell. It's as if an emotional dam broke up. I could feel the hot electricity flowing between us; it burned like the sun. I reluctantly broke away from him. We both gasped for air, which made me feel less embarrassed. Even though Hunter was the second boy I'd kissed, I knew the feelings weren't normal. None of the books I had read mentioned a feeling of this intensity. Unsure of how to process my emotions, I ran back to the house without a second thought. I thought that I heard him calling me in the distance, but I couldn't be sure.

I kept running until I reached my room. I quickly locked the door to keep myself from running back to him. Missing Themar, I thanked The Core that I only had several days before I returned to the Cloudarians. In the same breath, I was not sure how I would be able to handle being so far from Hunter. It felt like there was a magnetic field drawing us together. Remembering Themar's last words, I figured that I might have used the energy between Hunter and me to break his spell. On the next day, I decided to find him to make sure that the spell had been broken.

I woke up to the wonderful smell of what I thought was pastries and coffee. I jumped out of bed and threw on a t-shirt and some cut off shorts and ran downstairs. When I saw Hunter, I took a deep breath. He had a snug grey V-neck shirt that complimented his biceps. I bit my lip! Hunter cleared his throat, snapping me out of my trance. "Good morning," Daisy said, with a wandering smile. I smiled quickly, averting my eyes from their gaze, and started fixing a plate. I took a seat across from Hunter. We did not speak to each other. When breakfast was over, Hunter left to go to town. I took the opportunity to break Daisy's spell. As soon as I spoke the words, "tumeish-youzerith," Daisy began to gasp for air as if she had been holding her breath for a long time. When she gained her composure, she wrapped her arms around me, thanking me. "I've been trying to break the spell for the last six months. It was as if there was a block on any information regarding the keeper's ordinance. We have a lot to talk about. You may want to take a seat. I will make some tea," she said as she left for the kitchen.

While Daisy was making the tea, Hunter returned and entered the room. I began to apologize. He stopped me! "It is okay! Last night was intense for me as well. However, we must explore our emotions while I still feel a strange connection to you," he said. However, I said nothing because the look on his face left no room for an argument. I admitted to myself that I was also curious. Daisy returned with the tea, and she re-directed our conversation to the matter at hand. Hunter explained to Daisy and me that he was under a spell by King Con, the king of Lidarians. I almost choked on my tea, shocked by his words. Hunter said his mission was to get close to me to gain my trust. Once he got me to let down my guard, he was to incapacitate me and bring me to an undisclosed location. I was unsure of any further plans. I asked, "Does he know that your spell has been broken?" "I do not think so, because I was contacted yesterday. Somehow our communication link was not severed," Hunter answered. I was relieved to hear this bit of news since we could use it to our advantage. I wondered how much Latherius knew about his father's plan. Hunter brought his hand to my face, massaging my worry lines, and I relaxed. Even though he was a human, there was something magical about his touch. I thought about what King Con was willing to do to me.

Now, I was ready to get to work. I instructed Hunter to get comfortable and lie on the couch for me to read his mind. I was hoping by hacking into his link with King Con that I could splice the link to contact someone I trusted. He didn't look too pleased, but he complied with my request. I told Daisy I would call her if I needed any help. I asked Hunter to empty his mind by thinking of a peaceful place and recalling as many details as possible. I assured him that it would lessen his resistance to my intrusion. Finally, when I felt his mental barrier decreasing, I began to search his mind for a connection. It took a couple of hours, but I found it.

Someone cleverly disguised it as a neuron. I spliced the connection to King Con, not cutting it completely so that he wouldn't get suspicious. Before I secured the secondary link, I warned Hunter that he might suffer a severe headache. He gritted his teeth and slightly nodded. His curly blonde hair fell into his eyes. I brushed his hair backward and slowly kissed his neck to distract him. I quickly secured the link, and he gasped for air but did not scream. I wanted to comfort him, but there was no time. I thrust energy into him and secured a connection with Bilow. I gave Bilow a brief explanation regarding what had transpired since we last spoke. He responded, knowing how painful it must have been for Hunter. "You and the human will have access to the portal tomorrow at dawn. Use the U-wave to access the link and make sure you hold on tight to the human. I should be able to transport both of you safely simultaneously," Bilow said. He broke our link. I rubbed Hunter's back as he struggled to stabilize his breathing. We ate and updated Daisy. He packed a light bag, and we decided to get some rest.

CHAPTER 9

The Unexpected Invasion

---

*H*unter was startled when I woke him up. Yet, he quickly regained his composure. We ate a quick snack and said our goodbyes to Daisy. She took Hunter into her arms and looked at him sternly. "If you get into trouble, you may be a human, but you are stronger than you know. I am beginning to believe that there is some truth in our ancient folklore, and truth lies with you two," Daisy said to him. He nodded and gave her bear hug, and we left. To make up some time, we took his truck to a nearby access point in the woods. Well, I told him it was to make up time, but the truth was that I didn't care about encountering those slithering creatures that lived in woods. The thought of those creatures caused me to shake. I assured him that I was okay. "Just caught a chill," I said. Once we arrived at the portal entrance, I was in awe of the beautiful stars and the huge new moon. It was a sight that I had committed to memory from my studies. We stepped to the access point with minutes to spare. Hunter grabbed me gently and whispered, "If I don't make it, I don't want you to have any regrets. I'm falling in love with you, and I want you to know I would die for you." He rubbed my arms, and I got goose bumps. With seconds left, I gave him a quick kiss, and he wrapped his arms tightly around me. I used my energy to open the U-wave frequency at exactly 12:00 am as the effort caused my body to shake. The portal opened, and I began to lift off the ground slowly. The pressure pulled me upward; however, Hunter's body was not lifted. He screamed! I held to his hands tightly. My body was in a vertical position, and at the last minute, the pressure intensified. Suddenly, Hunter's body attached to me like a magnet. Vibrant lights surrounded us, swirling in the most beautiful pattern. We came to an abrupt stop.

Disoriented, we both fell to the ground. After a couple of minutes, my vision cleared, and I saw Hunter looking at me with a strange look. "What?" I asked him. "You are so beautiful," he replied. To me, it was a strange thing to say at the moment. I saw my hands. I looked different. My eyes had returned to a lavender color, and my skin was slightly translucent. Looking uncomfortable, I said, "I really didn't pay much attention to my human form other than the first day that I arrived. I may have forgotten to mention to you what I looked like as a Cloudarian." "You are beautiful," Hunter said. I was thankful that he stopped me from rambling. "Thank you," I said, flattered and embarrassed. He brought his hand toward my face and stopped. He noticed that his skin as changing to a milky translucent color. I held my breath for his response. He gave me a crooked smile. "If you think that I'm hot, I don't care. I don't mind the change," he said. I burst out laughing, and it broke the tension. Finally, I was able to focus and look around and identify our location. We were in the all too familiar cave wall, Billow's layer.

The name was a joke among the students, and it stuck. The name was due to the mysteriousness of its design as well as Bilow's mysterious pet, Irout. Irout was a creature created from the beginning of time. He was the only creature who could die and be reborn. Each rebirth had a slightly different personality but carried the same memories of its previous existence. All I knew was that the creature served as some sort of energy source for the seers' powers. I signaled for Hunter to follow me closely, not knowing if Bilow's layer was compromised. Although it was highly unlikely due to his energy dome protecting his layer— no one with malicious intent could penetrate the layer. Hearing a noise, I placed a finger over my mouth to keep quiet. We pressed our back against the wall of the layer. We walked backward slowly toward the living quarters where the noise seemed to be. We entered the living quarter. I was always taken aback by Bilow's abrasive scary décor of blackish gray walls, with silver accents, with a contrast of all his white furniture. Finally, locating the noise, I ran and fell to the floor next to Bilow's limped body.

I shook him hard, and thankfully, his eyes opened slowly. "What happened to you?" I asked Bilow. "My lovely girl, I passed out from the stress of transporting you and your human," he replied. He looked fatigued, but he was pleased with himself. "Help me to my chambers. I need to rest," he obliged me. His pet, Irout, entered the room with some weird energy, moving too quickly for my comfort. Hunter moved closer to me in a protective stance. I placed my hand in his hand to calm him. Mentally, I faulted myself for not warning Hunter about Bilow's pet's protective nature.

Irouts were short but had a very muscular frame with pointy ears and sharp teeth. Hunter whispered to me from the side of his mouth, "Is he safe?" I laughed and assured Hunter that it would not harm us, and he began to relax. Irout left the room as fast as it entered while uttering to Bilow in a weird sounding native tongue. A seer like Bilow could only understand its sound. Hunter and I lifted Bilow to his feet and walked him through a rustic kitchen to his chambers. Feeling uneasy in his private chambers, we led him to his colossal round bed. Once he's seated at the edge of his bed, I removed his shoes, and he lay down. I pulled the covers over him, and we left him to rest. Also, I began to feel the effects of the events, so I led Hunter to one of the guest chambers. However, I barely reached the bed before I passed out.

I woke up dumbfounded. I was disoriented. It took a minute to realize what Bilow was yelling at me. "Hurry! Engage your beam-matter gun! We have a breach. Meet us in the training room!" he yelled. Once Bilow turned to leave, I quickly shifted into my combat gear and engaged my weapon. I followed closely behind Bilow. My senses were on high alert. Finally, we reached the training quarters, and I ran toward Hunter and Themar. "I need you all to listen to me; your life depends on it. Airea, I need you to lead the others to the emergency escape room. There is a spell that I need cast to disorient the invaders. Keep straight, no matter what obstacles you encounter. I'm not sure how anyone could have penetrated my wards. My best guess is that it has something to do with Hunter's presence. I am going to provide a distraction so you all can escape," Bilow instructed. "Remember my proficiency," he whispered in my ear. "You'll hear my signal. Don't leave this room until you do," he added. With an unusual hug, he nodded at me and took off. With an uneasy feeling, I distracted myself by showing Themar and Hunter my beam-matter gun. Themar controlled her expression and took the gun with a look of determination. Hunter grabbed the gun with one hand and grabbed my hand with his other hand, and then brought the gun to his lips. "I will protect you with my life," he said and gave me a light kiss. It hardened my resolve. "What about me?" Themar asked. "You will protect me, too, right?" Breaking the tension, Hunter said, "I believe you two are a package deal. Plus, Airea will kill me if I let something happen to you. I don't want to be a dead hero." We settled down and waited at the door, listening carefully as we expected Bilow's signal.

A Journey to the Core

I opened the door as soon as I heard a loud blast from the east wing. I led everyone westward through a secret passageway that had left and right turns. We hastened our pace as we felt the ground trembling from consecutive blasts. I prayed to the Core for Bilow's protection. We finally reached our destination, and we held hands walking through the translucent wall together.

As soon as we walked through the wall, the scene before us changed. I instantly recognized that we were in a place that humans would call a jungle. I could feel unbearable humidity. Having not felt the effects of humidity in the Cloudarian, Themar required couching to adjust her breathing. She caught her breath, and we continued our journey. Hunter took the lead, and I took up the rear. We walked up steep terrain. Under different circumstances, I would've marveled at the sight. We kept on a straight path until we reached a cliff overlooking a lake. Confused, Hunter arched his eyebrow and said, "Bilow did say we should remain straight despite the obstacle." "It might be a good time to mention that I don't know how to swim, and we can't fly in this strange place," Themar exclaimed in frustration. I quickly dismissed the possibility of oversight on Bilow's instructions.

In all the chaos, while Themar debated our options, I decided to trust Bilow. So, I jumped off the cliff. I suppressed my scream, and instead of falling into the lake, I landed on solid ground. Unable to hear or see my friends, I waited for them for what seemed to be ten minutes before I heard Themar scream. Once she realized where she had landed, she opened her eyes. She realized that she was on solid ground. She abruptly let loose Hunter's hand and hit him. She yelled: "I can't believe you pushed me off the cliff." Not really worried about Hunter, but wanting to keep moving, I intervened. I explained to her that Hunter probably knew that she would not jump willingly. Graciously, Themar accepted my explanation, glared at Hunter, turned, and began to walk ahead of us. Hunter squeezed my hand and thanked me for coming to his rescue. Themar yelled over her shoulder, "Are you love birds coming or not?" I felt my cheeks turning red with embarrassment. So, I turned from Hunter and quickly followed

Themar. Mentally, I was hoping that he didn't catch my feelings of embarrassment. If he did, I was thankful that he didn't say anything as he followed me.

The elevation of the hill changed and began to walk downhill. I began to relax my mind, but I wondered about Bilow. I'd never had to worry about him with his foresight. I had always assumed that he would be able to anticipate any possible attack. I had always assumed that he would die a natural life cycle. His natural life cycle did not end for another century. It would take a century for another seer to acquire all his knowledge. We never anticipated that bringing a human into our realm could somehow cloud his vision. Lost in thought, I bumped into Themar. Before I saw Hunter waving at us, I asked her, "Why did you stop so abruptly?" We moved back behind a nearby tree, and Hunter signaled for us to remain quiet. I finally saw what had gotten their attention. It appeared to be a pack of fanatical dogs. Naively, I walked toward the pack of dogs. As I passed the angry dogs, I was blinded. I blinked my eyes to clear my sight; however, I could only see darkness. I flexed my hand, and I felt relieved; even though I couldn't see myself, I could feel my body. Somehow that realization helped to slow my escalating panic. Minutes later, I heard Hunter's voice calling my name. "Hunter, Hunter, I'm here!" I yelled back. "Don't move from where you are!" he said. "Stretch out your hands to see if we can touch each other," he added. At first, I felt nothing. As I was about to tell him, I felt his hand moving up my thighs, which caused a burning electrical sensation moving through my body. I released a soft gasp and quickly grabbed his hand. Once we heard Themar's voice, we proceeded with our stretched-out hands to locate her. With our hands interlocked, we navigated one step at a time in sync through the empty space. It was very disorienting to feel our body without seeing it. Our depth perception was completely off-center. Finally, we made it out of the maze with no help from Themar. That girl might have been more trouble than the illusion!

Once we escaped the place of illusion, we entered a clearing that led us to a medieval cathedral. It was fully equipped with a draw bridge, moot, and alligators. I recalled the place from my stored memories. Hunter crossed the bridge with his chest puffed out as if to restore his pride. Themar and I suppressed our laughter and followed closely behind him. We arrive at the colossal door, and Hunter attempted to open it, but the door didn't budge. "Now what?" Themar asked. I reached for the doorknob, and Themar rolled her eyes. At first, nothing happened, but right before I let go, I felt a tug and a sharp stinging sensation on the palm of my hand. As soon as the stinging sensation was gone, the door made a low humming noise and clicked open. As soon as we entered, we all jumped simultaneously when the door abruptly closed behind us. We jumped again when a short stumpy man appeared before us. He looked as old as the medieval castle. He had orange-reddish hair that was in stark contrast to his dark complexion. "Welcome, young ones. My name is Youf. Let me show you to your chambers. I can detect a severe level of fatigue. Once you are rested, I will answer all your questions," the man said. I looked at Hunter and felt terrible when I saw dark shadows under his eyes. Humans need more rest and nourishment than Cloudarians. We were shown to our chambers, and thankfully, we were all on the same floor. Restless, I tossed and turned. Every time I closed my eyes, I saw Billow's face. I was filled with so many emotions. Just as I decided to give up on sleep, I heard a soft knock on the door. So, I readied my defenses. Before I asked who it was, the door opened, and it was Hunter. I relaxed. Hunter looked tired and fine. He was wearing loose-fitted grey pants with no shirt. I assumed that our host provided the pants. He caught me viewing every inch of his body and cleared his throat. I stepped aside, and he walked into my room. "Sorry, I did not mean to wake you," Hunter said, courteously. I passively ignored his comments. "Would it be okay for me to sleep next to you tonight?" he asked. Not trusting my voice, I waved my arm toward the bed. We settled in bed. I felt his soft hair tickle my neck, but I dared not move. Probably aware of our proximity, he placed his warm left hand on my thigh.

"We never really got a chance to talk about what happened between us back at Daisy's house. How did our kiss break my spell? It has been crazy since I met you. It is driving me crazy, not being able to talk about us," he whispered in my ear. My whole body flushed as he lightly brushed his lips on my ear. "What is this electrical sensation between us? Do you feel it?" I sighed and turned toward him to regain my poise. It didn't help, but I finally spoke: "Well, Bilow told me that he had a theory about you. He believes that you may have more than human DNA in your linage." When Hunter heard my explanation, he had a blank stare. So, I decided to continue the conversation: "Bilow had planned to do a full diagnostic test on you. However, he did not have a chance to do it." "I am interested in knowing my linage. I gave up hope a long time ago. I would always run into obstacles. I attempted many times to find my biological parents. Daisy practically raised me, but she has never shared with me anything about my parents," Hunter said.

I swatted at what I thought was a fly. When I heard a deep baritone voice coming from what I had thought was a fly, I realized my mistake. "Hey, what are you trying to do, kill me?" the voice asked. "No, no, no! I thought you were a fly. My apologies!" "The name is Vos," the voice said again. "We are pleased to meet you," I said. "If that's how you greet people, I'm afraid for your enemies," he replied with a raspy baritone. His minuscule size, coupled with a big voice, big personality, and wiry orange hair, caused my vocal cord to form a laugh. I had a long history of laughing at the most inappropriate circumstances. Somehow, I managed to hold my laugh this time. "What are you?" Hunter blurted out before thinking. "The better question would be: Who created me and what for?" the strange creature exclaimed. "Anyhow, my name is Vos. Now, follow me," he said. I tripped in an attempt to run after the little fairy, with Hunter in tow. We sprinted down the winding passageway. "Slow down!" Hunter breathlessly cried out, and Voss slowed down. We approached a colossal medieval-looking door. I recalled Bilow telling me about a mysterious door that I would need to open. He assured me that I would know what to do. However, if I chose the wrong door, I would be forever sealed. Vos gestured toward Hunter to open the door. Hunter paused! He looked nervous, but with a shaking hand, he turned the knob.

However, nothing happened, and we all looked at one another in dismay. Hunter was unable to release the doorknob, and he began to panic. When the door apparently pricked him, he yelled. Suddenly, the door started to grow, and the designs on the door began to move. The door eventually opened, and Hunter released his hand from the door. We took baby steps forward into the entrance. Casually, Vos flew past us into the dark, damp room. He spoke some unintelligible words, and the torches spontaneously lit themselves. Vos smiled, looking proud of himself. The room was empty except for an old tree trunk. Assuming it would open, Hunter touched it. When nothing happened, he waved his hands and dropped them to his sides. "Maybe both of you must touch it," Vos said. Figuring it couldn't hurt, we both touched the tree trunk, and it started to vibrate. Branches and leaves shot out from the trunk. I stepped backward, bringing Hunter with me. "Whoop! It feels fantastic to spread my branches," an alto female voice spoke from the tree trunk. Her image was carved in the center of the trunk. "My name is

Airea, and this is Hunter," I said. Looking irritated, the fairy said, "I am Vos. It's a pleasure to make your acquaintance." "My name is Midgle," the female voice said. "What can I do for you, children?" Looking at Vos, I laughed to myself at his seething expression at being called a child. "We were hoping that you could tell us Hunter's linage. We are curious about his ability to enter this realm as a human," I said to Midgle.

Midgle began talking to us. I was tired, but I did my best to follow her conversation. I tried not to show it, but I felt like, if I had the opportunity, I would be able to sleep for days. I tried not to let it show, but her lengthy conversation affected me physically.

Hunter and I grabbed hold of her by the branches on both sides of her trunk. Understanding our intent, she extended her branches. Midgle closed her eyes. In an instant, we were transported to an unfamiliar land. It had the resemblance of the rainforest on earth. It was impressive: large leafy trees were wandering through it. The trees were walking! Instantly, I recognized Midgle. She was a few feet from me. As if she read my thoughts, she waited until I had calmed my nerves.

"I know you are disoriented, child, but there isn't much time. Follow me quickly! I have covered you and Hunter with a shield, so they can't see or detect you. We must hurry because it won't hold long," Midgle said.

As I followed Midgle through the forest, the hairs on my neck stood up. Every time we passed a tree, it sniffed the air, scanning its surrounding as if it felt there was something amiss. Almost tripping over a large branch, I decided it's probably best to focus on avoiding a scene.

Thankfully, Midgle slowed her pace. I saw a rock formation. It didn't appear like she saw the rocky formation. In shock, I couldn't speak to warn her in time. She collided with the rocky formation. At that point of impact, she vanished.

We ran toward the rock formation where she vanished. However, Hunter ended up with a severe headache from running into the rock. A few seconds later, we saw a branch protruding from a rock. Cautiously, we grabbed hold of the branch, and I felt a sharp tug. We got pulled through the rock quickly. We came out on the other side of the rocky formation. Hunter tripped over his feet, and Midgle caught him before he could fall to the ground. As if that was not bad enough, she laughed at him. "Sorry, child, I forgot humans have poor balance," Midgle said.

Hunter picked up his pride, and we followed Midgle deeper into the magnificent realm. It had colorfully laminated gems embedded into its walls. The gems helped to light our path. I saw what appeared to be a glittering waterfall. Midgle gestured for us to walk into the glittering reservoir. It looked shallow enough that I could stand from the deepest point. Considering everything we had done and witnessed thus far, it didn't seem unreasonable. We stepped into the water; it was freezing, and it felt more like slime than water. Midgle gestured for us to move deeper, and I kept walking until I could barely stand. Shivering from the cold, I could hardly speak. Not to mention, I didn't care to ingest the substance. "I better not be shining when I get out of here," I said to myself. As soon as I finished that thought, I felt something moving around my legs. It wrapped itself around us and tugged at our legs. I cried out to Midgle! When I noticed she didn't lift a branch to help us, I felt the pain of betrayal. I barely got a chance to breathe before we were tugged under. We traveled downward at a rapid speed. I could no longer hold my breath. Before I lost conscious-ness, the slime was gone. We entered a large air bubble.

Hunter heaved and gasped for air. One of the biggest fear of humans was drowning to death. As Hunter was filling his lungs with air, I tried to shake off my panic attack. I noticed three gas-like figures. "What now?" I threw my arms in the air. I was afraid that I was losing my mind.

"My apologies! We are sorry you've had to endure such a rough journey," a voice said. I couldn't hear them with my ears, but I could hear them in my head. Surprisingly, it wasn't unpleasant. They all had different tones, yet they spoke at the same time, and the result was harmonious and hypnotizing.

They said to Hunter, "Do you know who we are, son?" He shook his head in the negative, obviously afraid to speak. "We are the Core!" the voice said. His legs trembled, and he fell to his knees. "Rise, son!" the voice encouraged. Hunter staggered to his feet, with trepidation and shaky hands. The Core addressed us thus:

We have seen many unsettling things and many beautiful things humans have accomplished over the centuries. There are few who are blinded by hate and jealousy and would like to destroy the humans. We have no choice. We must intervene. We know you have questions you would want to ask, but there is no time for that now. It is as you suspect, child: you are more than human. You are half Lidarian. Your father was a Lidarian. He fell in love with your mother while on a mission to earth. They were banished from earth because they broke the rules. Your mother's memory of her Lidarian lover and your memory of her were destroyed. This may sound cruel, but we must remain a secret from humans to maintain a balance of our two worlds. You were placed in the care of keepers. You were brought here so we could unleash a special gift you have hidden inside of you. When you wake, you will think that this is a dream. You will know that it is not a dream because you will realize that the electricity in you has been intensified. You'll be instructed on how to use it, and you will know when to use it. Sleep, my children!

We woke up, and we were where we started, the mystical castle.

In the following weeks, Hunter spent his time with Midgle being trained on how to use and control his powers. Vos volunteered to be

Hunter's moving target. The first couple of days, Vos was amused by his ability to taunt Hunter's poor aim. However, toward the end of the week, the roles reversed as Hunter's aim improved significantly. Themar and I used their training sessions for our entertainment. By the end of the week, Vos quit and threatened to sue for damages. We all burst out in laughter. Breaking through his otherwise serious demeanor, Youf smiled at Vos' threats.

Youf notified Themar, Hunter, and me that our presence was required in Midgle's chambers. As soon as we arrived in the middle of the chambers, she woke up from one of her many naps. "Oh, there you are, children. I am afraid that our time together has come to an end," Midgle told us. About an hour later, we left her chambers with our mission from the Core. We were honored and nervous about serving the Core.

We began packing our items to prepare for the journey back to Bilow's layer. Midgle assured us that we were safe under the new seer's protection. I requested bottled water and food for our journey back to Bilow's layer. Midgle said, "It is not required." Realizing that I did not understand her meaning, she explained: "We will teleport all three of you at once."

Truth and Its Consequences

When Hunter sighed behind me, I jumped at the sound of his voice. I had not heard his voice since we returned from our trip with Midgle. He had not shared with me his emotions of learning about his linage at the moment. However, I was sure he would in his own time. Since our descent was somewhat painful for Hunter, I had concerns about our ascent. Hunter assured me that he could handle our ascent. Themar was delighted that we were being teleported back to the Cloudarian.

After being teleported, it took me a minute to figure out where I was. I recognized my surroundings. Even though it looked different, I was lying on the floor of Bilow's living quarters. The structure of the room was the same. Instead of the subtle earth tones, there were splashes of emerald green everywhere. It took me a moment to gather my composure.

Hunter, Themar, and I were in different rooms throughout Bilow's layer. Within minutes, I met Hundu. Hund was the new seer. It took me some time to accept the idea that Bilow was gone. Yet, Hundu was all we had. We went over the events that took place during our jump through the portal to the Core. We made sure to leave nothing out, knowing that Hundu was a new seer.

Hundu gave Themar and me instructions to gather intel and ask us to meet him in Bilow's command room. Hunter protested Hundu's decision for him to remain behind but eventually gave in to his logic. Hundu believed that my life might be put in danger if Hunter and I were to be together. Before I left, I set aside some time for Hunter and me. With all that had taken place, we needed some time alone.

As soon as we entered a private room and I closed the door, Hunter grabbed me, and our lips touched. Once we embraced, I felt a familiar energy surge, but this time, it was more intense. Suddenly, he jumped back. "Are you okay?" Hunter said. "I need to learn how to control my emotions around you. The powers that the Core gave me proved to be hard to control, especially when my emotions are heightened. I don't want to hurt you. Now, I know why things have felt different since his interaction with the Core," explained. I assured him that he would not hurt me. Looking skeptical, he agreed to let his guard down.

The Sacrifice of Being Privileged

On the following day, I gathered my nerves before meeting with Latherius, unsure of what to expect. I did not know if he was aware of his father's plans to infiltrate the rank of the seers. I did not know if he was part of the group that attacked Bilow's layer. I resisted the urge to fiddle with my hands as Hunter did when he nervous.

Upon my arrival at Latherius' office, while waiting for him, his secretary looked at me when she thought I was not paying her any attention. She seemed to be sizing me up. She was a pretty young Cloudarian. Cloudarian women could change their hair color and length and body shape in an instant but were unable to change their facial features or eye colors. Her eyes were a rare and stunning shade of purple. Her haircut was a shoulder-length bob-cut. I wondered if she was Latherius' old or current conquest in my absence.

I felt a chill in my spine when I heard his voice while moving down the corridor. He spoke to the secretary and then looked my way. With a wild smile on his face, he ran across the room, picked me up, and gave me an intense hug. Stunned by his reaction, I was left speech-less and stiff. Finally, I snapped out of it and returned his embrace. He looked as if he had aged since our last time together. He put me down and looked at me as if he was reading my mind. After several awkward moments passed, he guided me to his office.

"Not that I'm not glad to see you, but what brings you to this neck of the woods?" he said. Latherius could speak humans' vernacular effortlessly, and it always impressed me. I gave him my rehearsed explanation, and he seemed to accept it without question. We agreed to meet for dinner later that afternoon.

I arrived at the place that he had given me. I was somewhat shocked that the location was a residence instead of a restaurant, as I had assumed. It was a beautiful white estate. When I approached the door, it automatically opened. Feeling a bit exposed, I cursed Themar for making me wear a backless, black, silk dress. I took a deep breath and entered the house.

The house interior was modern with shades of grey and black with maroon accents.

Fireplaces throughout the house gave it a romantic esthetic. "Welcome to my humble abode," he said. I snorted at that remark. A bad habit I picked up from Daisy. He took my hand and kissed it before leading me to the dining room.

The kitchen staff served our meal, and every course was better than the previous one. The meal was delicious, and I had my fill. I was thankful to the Core that our weight or shape did change after our maturity date. He looked at me and said, "I'm not going to lie. I was starting to believe that I wouldn't see you again, especially since you haven't reached out to me since your return to the Cloudarian." Taking aback by his comment, the hairs on my neck stood up. "I did not make any public appearance until two days ago. I decided to spend some time with my parents," I replied. I considered my best option was to deflect his conversation, so, I changed the subject. I directed the conversation on the subject matter that I was sent to retrieve.

He asked me to follow him to the deck. We sat on the deck and watched the sunset. The view was different from this position. The sunset took my breath away. "Why did you come to see me?" he asked, breaking my daydream. "Um! I missed you. Can't I catch up with a friend? Or are you not happy to see me?" I said, working hard to exhibit my best sad face. "Oh, no! I'm sorry; things have been a little crazy around here since you've been away. Everyone is on edge since Bilow's death," Latherius said. I gritted my teeth and remained silent, which forced him to give details. "My dad has been on edge. He is paranoid. He believes that whoever killed Bilow could be out for more blood," he added. It sounded like a guilty conscience to me, but

I kept that to myself. I attempted to get more information from him, but he did not volunteer any additional information about his father. We agreed to meet again, and I stood up to leave. Before I reached for the doorknob, he grabbed me firmly around my waist.

I woke up, blinking my eyes rapidly. The darkness had given way to a glimmer of light shining through a circle hole, mimicking a window. I could see the frigid air escaping my lips. I stretched my body to evaluate my surroundings and injury. Thankfully, I didn't sense any injury, just some soreness. The moonlight, as well as my minimal soreness, told me I'd been unconscious for several hours. As I took note of my surroundings, I saw an old metal toilet tucked in the back corner of my cell. A jug of water was in my cell, too. I took a deep breath, to bring my anxiety under control. I tried to clear my foggy mind. "That bastard must have drugged me!" was the last thought that ran through my mind before I lost consciousness again.

I was wakened in shock when I felt cold water splashing on my face and torso. "You will have to forgive my impatience. I could not wait any longer for you to wake up, my dear. Kindly accept my apologies for my son's ignorance. When I told him to keep you in a secured location, I certainly did not mean a dungeon with no accommodations!" I heard someone say. I opened my eyes to see none other than King Con. He sat in a gold chair that was a ridiculous contrast to the environment of the dungeon. I struggled to get to my feet and sit in the golden chair that he had for me to sit. Latherius looked at me but did not move from the corner of the cell, where he perched his leg against the wall.

He looked away to avoid my gaze. "Get her some water!" he snapped. He handed me the glass, still avoiding my stare. "What a coward!" I thought to myself. I could not believe I entertained thoughts of being with him.

"So, I bet you are wondering why you are here under these circumstances," King Con said, as he entered. I said nothing to that. I just kept my face blank, reminding myself of my hostage training. "I like this girl; she is cool, even under pressure," he said, laughing. "Well!" he clapped his hands, "Let's not drag this out. She is a pretty girl! You are too young to remember, but long ago, the Lidarians' tribe was a respected and feared people. Until a Lidarian named Turin, a flogger, not unlike yourself, went to earth and fell in love with a beautiful human woman. Against the advice of his elders, he brought the human home. She was not a good person. It took a while, but finally, Turin saw the error of his ways. Unfortunately, by then it was too late. Turin was banished back to earth to live out the remainder of his life as a human. Only the elders know the transgressions of the past; nevertheless, the past hunts our legacy. A marriage between the most eligible princess and the prince would restore our legacy. Since I know you didn't know what you were doing, I'm willing to keep a secret. That's the secret of Hunter. That is if you are willing to marry my son and if you want your boyfriend to live. That's right! I forgot to mention," he twisted his leg in laughter and continued, "Turin was banished to earth, but the human was sentenced to death." I controlled my expression, knowing he's expecting a reaction. I was determined not to give him that pleasure. I did everything I could to not frown at Latherius when he pretended not to be looking at me. "I'll give you one day to make your decision," said

King Con. "Make sure you give her more suitable accommodations," he yelled over his shoulder as he walked out the cell.

The next morning, I was awakened by the aroma of coffee. I jumped up with joy as coffee had become a delicacy for me since my stay with Daisy. On remembering where I was, the euphoria dissipated. Even though I was fully dressed, I pulled my blanket over my shoulders. I saw Latherius sitting at the table on the balcony outside my door. The table was clearly set for two. Before I lost my nerve, I hopped out of bed, and ran to the bathroom, freshened up, and went outside.

After exchanging fake pleasantries, we ate in awkward silence. The carefree flirting was gone. I broke the silence, saying, "So, are you willing to go through with this marriage because your father commands it? What if I say no, have you been commanded to kill me? Are you prepared to kill me?" I took a deep breath to calm my nerves. He said, "I wouldn't be able to kill you, and you know that." I laughed to myself. "That does not mean he would not contract someone else to kill me," he shot out. "What an honorable family you have!" I said sarcastically. He lowered his head slightly. I decided it would be beneficial to be nice to him rather than trying to get information from him.

"So, what is on the agenda for today? Is your assignment to convince me to marry you? Ha-ha!" I said, laughing. Noticeably, he did not like the joke because a sad expression floated across his face, but it was gone in an instant. "I'm not sure why this bothers me, but I'm a sucker for a sad case. If you are looking to have a good time, you are in luck," he said, overly excited, putting his hand out for me to take it.

However, I could tell that his behavior was unnatural. Yet, I decided to go with the flow, assuming that he was trying to lighten the mood.

Even though I asked many times, he wouldn't tell me our destination. Exhausted mentally and physically, I gave up asking him. It was a reasonable distance away. So, he decided that we should take his antique vessel. They had been around for about one century. Someone figured how to harness the power from The Core to power the vessels. "I was forced against my will to learn how to fly one of these death contraptions," he said. Even though they assured me there was no reason to need to operate it in a manual mode, I was glad that I learned how manually to operate it. The manual feature was the only reason I was convinced to get into one of the horrid things. I smiled at the thought of Themar, teasing me about my "irrational fear".

When I realized where we were going, I gasped, overwhelmed with excitement. I had to remind myself that I was essentially a prisoner. When I saw a replica of the annual Carnival in Rio, I tried not to show my excitement. The people dressed in colorful customs. There were exotic animal replications, fire-blowers, and what looked like real rollercoasters!

He said, "Just so you know, your every move is being monitored, in case you get any funny thoughts." I wondered if he was reading my mind, but I said nothing to him. "Do you think you could just put all the unpleasantries behind us? At least for tonight..." Latherius asked me. "By unpleasantries, do you mean drugging me, locking me in a dungeon, and trying to force me to marry you?" "Sure! Why not?" he said. It was not what I wanted to say, but I said okay. He let out one of his unusual bright smiles. Having gone through so much, I said to myself, "Why not? It could not hurt to let my hair my down. Could it?" We decided to ride a rollercoaster.

By the time we got on the second roller-coaster, I was unable to contain my excitement. Latherius looked as if he was genuinely having fun. Exhausted from screaming on the rides, we took a walk to one of the booths and ordered some salty and sweet treats. We walked as we ate, making small talks as we tried different treats. I reminded myself that Latherius was not to be trusted. Yet, I felt like I needed some fun. He said, "Had you not thought about marrying me?" "Yes, but as you know, a lot has changed since our time together," I shot back. "You mean since you met the human and picked him over your own kind?" he said, harshly scowling at me. I ignored him, trying to control my anger at his words. He sighed and said: "I'm sorry! I just don't understand how your feeling for me could change so fast." We walked in awkward silence.

"Can we head back?" I said, in a low and soft voice, but he didn't answer me. He threw his food in the trash and started to pull me hastily. I was not sure why he was pulling on me in that manner. So, I thought of discreetly notifying someone about my predicament, but for what I knew, the people could be working for the king.

Somehow, we ended up walking right into a parade. Latherius kept a tight grip on my wrist, and I was forced to keep up with his brisk pace, stumbling along the way. A heap of confetti was released on top of us and the crowd. I thought I heard him cursing, but I couldn't be sure because the band's music was loud. Then there was a loud bang, and I realized it's not part of the parade. When the ground shuttered, I felt him releasing his grip on my wrist. The crowd separated us, and I started running with the crowd to avoid being trampled. As I navigated myself out of the crowd, something or someone pulled me down.

As I attempted to get up, I recognized Hunter's face. "Come quickly!" Hunter said, and I took after him, running right on his heels. When he ran into an invisible object, I ran into him, too. Hunter pulled me into a car, and I gasped in shock, as I felt a hand pulling me backward.

"Let me go, Latherius!" I said to him as he pulled me back. "I will! You just calm down! I know you do not trust me, but you need me to come with you," he said. "We made it here without you; we will make it back without you!" Themar sneered. I wasn't sure I'd ever seen her that angry. "There is no time for this. My father planned to infatuate Bilow's layer, I mean the new seer's layer to extract the human and hold him hostage for his contingency plan," he said. Worried that we would all be caught, I wondered if Latherius was up to something. So, I decided that we could watch him closely and use him for information. We jumped into the vessel, and

Themar took off. Careful not to hit any of the people who were trying to escape from the rumbling of the ground, Themar dodged and weaved to avoid hitting anyone while drawing attention to us.

"Um, now that we can't go back to Hundu's place, where are we going?" Themar remarked, soundings irritated. I was sure that her foul mood had to do with our uninvited guest. "Until we strategize your next plan, you can hide out in the old combat training center," Latherius replied. "Does anybody else have a better plan?" Themar asked. I racked my brain, trying to figure out another option. I was not too keen on taking any suggestions from Latherius, and since Hunter had only been there for a few days, it was up to me to determine the best place to hide. I searched my photographic memory of every place in that realm but came up with nothing that would not put other people at risk.

I reasoned that the best option was not in that realm.

We headed for the portal, and I could see the concern in Themar's face through the rear-view mirror. "If we use the portal to escape, won't they have security guarding it?" Hunter raised a legitimate point. We both turned and looked at Latherius, and he just shrugged. "It is highly likely that my father has surveillance around the portal in case you guys try to escape. I have no way of knowing until we get there because he does not disclose such information to me," Latherius said.

I decided it's worth the risk, not wanting to go anywhere upon Latherius's recommenda-tion. For some reason, I wanted to trust him against all rationale, but the question was, "How can I trust him, knowing the things he has done to me?" Finally, we arrived at the portal. I let out a breath that I didn't know I was holding.

"So, what are we doing here?" Themar asked, looking exhausted. "Hunter and I will return to earth, and I will come up with a plan from there. I believe it was a mistake bringing Hunter here," I said. "You are coming back, right?" Themar asked, looking desperate. "I can't lose you," she said. Refusing to lie to my best friend, I told her that I was unsure of what I was going to do. "We need to hurry; I'm not sure how long it will take for them to catch up to us," I told them.

"Silly children, did you really think that I would leave your only escape route unattended?" King Con said, with his eerie smile. "Son, I'm very disappointed in you. Did you really think that I would trust you with my prize possession without having a way to track you?" he said to Latherius. He clapped his hands, and a sharp bolt of lightning shot right through Latherius's body within several feet from us. Latherius' body laid limp on the ground. Furiously, I made to run toward him, but Hunter held me in place. "How could you do this to your flesh and blood? He's a traitor!" Latherius said. From where I was, I could see his body shaking in anger. I fell back slightly, not wanting to get my friends killed.

"Now, what shall I do with the rest of you?" King Con yelled. Hunter, my brave boy-friend, stepped in front of Themar and me. I was taken aback by his act of bravery. King Con said to Themar, "Maybe you can come up with a suitable punishment. Aren't you a judge? Well, that wouldn't be fair for you to decide your own fate!" Tired of being toyed with, I interrupted his rambling: "If you take Latherius to the healer before it is too late, I will marry him."

Hunter turned toward me in protest. With a twitch of his wrist, King Con tossed Hunter through the air, and he landed near Latherius. Thankfully, he seemed unhurt. He attempted to get up but was held down by an invisible force.

King Con cocked his head as he was perplexed at the unusual motion of Hunter's body. Whatever Hunter was doing, his body was shaking from the effort. Themar slipped a silver object into my hand. I recognized it instantly as the cortical spear. It was considered the only weapon that could end our life source. I had only seen them in history books, so I was confused about what to do with the spear. It was not wise to use it on King Con. "If I kill him without an heir apparent, unimaginable lightning storm will hit the earth with catastrophic results until a successor is named," I said to myself. The last leader whose life force ended was due to natural causes. This was centuries ago. According to our history books, the brief naming of a successor caused several tornados throughout South America. The leader of each tribe maintained a delicate atmospheric balance of the earth.

"Bilow said, 'You would know what to do

when the time came for you to make a life or death decision,'" Themar reminded me. In that instant, I knew what I must do. I hugged my best friend and turned to Hunter. I was so proud of him standing up to King Con! I yelled as loud as my voice could allow me and got King Con's attention. He cast Hunter to the ground and held him there as if he were toying with him.

"It is me you want, right?" I asked, but he said nothing. "Did anyone ever tell you that you cannot have what is not yours?" I asked again and then aimed the spear to my heart and released it and its power. I felt my life force fading, and I prayed that The Core might accept my sacrifice and spare the ones I loved.